This book belongs to

....

Written by Alexandra Robinson.
Illustrated by Clare Fennell.

Little Reindeer's Christmas Wish

Clare Fennell • Alexandra Robinson

make
believe
ideas

Far away, in Christmas Town,
a reindeer had a dream:
to fly with Santa's Festive Fleet –
the coolest reindeer team.

Each year, he'd watch the team soar off
and **marvel** at the sight.
"One day, when both my **antlers grow**,
I'll get to join their flight!"

But Little Reindeer's antlers
just never **ever** grew,
and though he'd **wait** . . .

and **wait** . . .

Will my
antlers
ever grow?

age 5 6

They STILL
haven't
grown!

and wait . . .

no antlers would come through.

As Christmas Eve was dawning,
the **Festive Fleet** prepared.

They shined their **hooves**, tried on their **kits**
and got their **reins** repaired.

With his nose **pressed** on the window,
the small deer **gazed** inside.

He watched them hold their **antlers** high
and wear their **coats** with pride.

Little Reindeer gave a sigh,
then glumly trudged away.

He groaned,
"Why won't my antlers grow
so I can fly the sleigh?"

A friendly elf was standing near
and hearing this, he said:

"Why don't we **make** some antlers
you can wear upon your head?"

The little deer was overjoyed –
"**Great idea!**" he cried.

So, off they went to search for things
that might be **antler-sized**.

First, they looked in **Chestnut Wood** for **holly** they could pick.

OUCH!

But the leaves were **prickly**
and didn't do the trick!

Next, they got some **icy snow** from Christmas Town's main square.

At first the antlers **sparkled** . . .

then they **melted** everywhere!

With Mrs Claus, they baked a batch
of **antler gingerbread**.

FLOUR

But when they left it out to cool,
a **mouse** ate it instead.

Just then, they heard the chiming of the
Christmas Countdown Clock.

TIME TO FLY!

PACK SLEIGH

READ LETTERS

WRAP PRESENTS

WRITE NICE LIST

MAKE TOYS

It was time to wave off Santa
and his merry reindeer flock.

But Santa Claus was worried –
his Christmas sleigh was full:

"There are **far too many** presents
for the Festive Fleet to pull!"

"This year, my list has **grown** again,
with more good girls and boys.
I'll have to use my **second sleigh**
to carry all these toys."

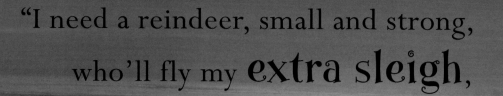

"I need a reindeer, small and strong,
who'll fly my **extra sleigh**,

to carry these last **Christmas gifts**
and get us on our way."

Suddenly, the friendly elf
had a bright idea:

"Little Reindeer, you could help:
you should volunteer!"

The little deer stepped forward
and said **bravely** in reply:
"I could fly your **one-horse sleigh**
if you will let me try?"

Santa hugged the little deer,
declaring with delight:

"I'd **love** for you to
join the team and
fly with us **tonight!**"

So, Little Reindeer got his **wish** –
the **perfect** Christmas treat:
he flew an extra-special sleigh
and joined the **Festive Fleet!**

He learnt it didn't matter
that his **antlers** never grew.
He only needed **bravery**
to join the reindeer crew.

Arriving back on **Christmas Day,**
the team let out a cheer.

"Little Reindeer, you're the best! Please **fly** with us **next year!**"

Happy Christmas!